# THE WIZARDS OF WYRD WORLD

WAY-
TOO-REAL
ALIENS

#3

# THE WIZARDS OF WYRD WORLD

PAMELA F. SERVICE · ILLUSTRATIONS BY MIKE GORMAN

MINNEAPOLIS

Darby Creek
A division of Lerner Publishing Group, Inc.
241 First Avenue North
Minneapolis, MN 55401 U.S.A.

Website address: www.lernerbooks.com

Main body text set in ITC Officina Sans Std Book 12/18
Typeface provided by International Typeface Corp

Library of Congress Cataloging-in-Publication Data

Service, Pamela F.
    The wizards of Wyrd World / by Pamela F. Service ; illustrated by Mike Gorman.
        p.    cm. — (Way-too-real aliens ; #3)
    Summary: When aspiring author Josh Higgins learns that his favorite author is coming to town, he and his sister Maggie convince fantasy writer P.L. Cuthbertson to take them to the magical medieval land of Wyrd World, where they find real trouble.
    ISBN: 978-0-7613-7920-1 (trade hard cover : alk. paper)
    [1. Authors—Fiction. 2. Middle Ages—Fiction. 3. Extraterrestrial beings—Fiction. 4. Voyages and travels—Fiction. 5. Brothers and sisters—Fiction. 6. Science fiction.] I. Gorman, Mike, ill. II. Title.
PZ7.S4885Wj  2012
[Fic]—dc23                                                              2011041039

Manufactured in the United States of America
1 – SB – 7/15/12

FOR ELAINE
—P.S.

## CHAPTER ONE

# FAMOUS AUTHOR

"Hey, big brother," Maggie yelled as she burst into my bedroom, ignoring all the KEEP OUT signs. "Time to break out the alien gizmo!"

I coughed dramatically, even though my cold was getting better. "No way! Time for you to stop pestering me. We are *not* going to use that again." Leggy scurried off my pillow and perched on my bed's headboard to listen.

"But by staying home, you missed the announcement at school today," Maggie said. "They told us who this year's visiting author will be. P. L. Cuthbertson!"

I tried not to look as excited as I suddenly felt. P. L. Cuthbertson, my absolute favorite author. He writes the Wyrd World series. It's kind of medieval fantasy with an alien twist, lots of magic beasts and heroic warriors. Every book is a different adventure on this really crazy planet.

"Cool," I said, "but what does this have to do with the alien gizmo that we are *never* going to use again?"

"Don't you see? It's perfect. Cuthbertson's world would be so amazing to go to. We just have to plunk the device on his head and get him to think us there. In all his books, he's described Wyrd World in so much detail that we can't get into the kind of trouble we did the last couple times—in the worlds you wrote about."

Maybe I should explain a little. Last year, I won a school writing contest with a story about a world I thought I had made up. Then some nasty blue aliens— not from my story—showed up and explained that humans are one of the few species in the universe who write "fiction." At least we *think* it's fiction. What we really do is tune into worlds that exist somewhere else.

My story was set on a world where the blue aliens wanted to go. They'd hoped to steal some super mineral, and their gizmo—a silver circlet-thing they clamped around my head—took us all there. Maggie and I escaped the bad guys, helped some good guys, and finally got back home. Along with Leggy, a little alien beastie I'd picked up. A little later, Maggie talked me into writing about a perfect vacation world, which turned out to be anything but. After that, I vowed to never touch the circlet again. But this *was* tempting.

"It's too dangerous," I grumbled, ignoring Leggy's eager chirping. "Last time we could have been eaten, crushed, or drowned."

"That's because we were clueless about what we were getting into," Maggie said. "But in Cuthbertson's world there won't be any surprises. Just fun and adventure."

"Humph."

"Just think about it."

Unfortunately, I did.

. . .

It was nearly the end of the school year, and the

whole school was excited about the famous author's visit. Drawings based on his books covered the walls. All the classes had read something by him and made lists of questions. I reread all my favorites. Welcome banners swayed across the halls.

When the big day finally came, we were all herded into the assembly room. After a gushing introduction by our principal, P. L. Cuthbertson walked to the podium. Okay, so I was a little disappointed. Maybe I was expecting someone as heroic looking as his characters. He was short, scrawny, and kind of stooped forward. A wispy gray mustache sat on his upper lip like a sleepy caterpillar, and his eyes looked as big as an owl's as they blinked from behind thick, round glasses. Okay, I wear glasses too, but not such nerdy ones.

Cuthbertson talked like he was really tired, like he'd given this talk lots of times before. But he was still interesting. He'd written dozens more books besides his Wyrd World series, he noted. He used slides and a little laser pointer to talk about how he got the ideas for some of them. I had to chuckle to myself. I knew something that he didn't. He hadn't made up those worlds at all—he'd only described places that somewhere in the universe really existed.

When he talked about Wyrd World, I fingered the alien device that I'd crammed into my backpack. Maggie grinned at me from where she sat with her class. Her idea was stupid. I had no intention of actually doing it. Still, it couldn't hurt to bring the gizmo along, I figured.

The best part of the day was planned for after school. The teachers had chosen a half dozen kids who they considered the school's top writers to have an early dinner with the author. It was in the teachers' break room, not a fancy restaurant, but at least there were no teachers there. Just us and the author. Of course, Maggie snuck in too. I glared at her, but I had expected she'd do something like that.

The school had ordered in Chinese food. A row of Styrofoam containers sat open on the table. Cuthbertson quickly helped himself to some squid. Talk about alien-looking food!

"I hope we can be informal here," he sighed. "I'm tired and hungry and I don't feel like performing. Let's just talk."

A girl named Kirsten started. "All right. Mr. Cuthbertson . . ."

"Please, call me P.L."

"Okay, P.L. Do you do many of these school appearances?"

Spearing an egg roll with his chopsticks, he nodded. "Too many. Not that I don't like talking to kids. I do. But the visits are all so much the same. Cramped plane rides, assembly rooms that smell like floor polish, boring hotel rooms that all look alike. And it takes time away from my writing."

Jon, a guy I didn't know well, said, "But I bet the writing makes up for it. I mean, being able to create those awesome worlds and kind of live in them."

"Yeah, but that's a problem too. I don't have much of a *real* life. Sometimes I wonder if I spend too much time in the worlds I make up and not enough in this one. Now, if I could *really* spend time in those worlds, if I could really mingle with wizards and heroes . . . that would be worth it. But they don't exist, except in my imagination."

Maggie and I exchanged looks across the food-strewn table. I had noodles overflowing my mouth so she got to it first. "So, P.L., if you could really go to one of those planets—maybe Wyrd World—would you?"

He laughed. "In a heartbeat. But now we're talking *real* fantasy."

He went on to talk about his cats, how he dealt with writer's block, and boring stuff like contracts and royalties. I asked a few questions to be polite, but my mind was elsewhere. I thought about what I knew we shouldn't do and what we almost certainly would do. Or at least try to do.

After the last fortune cookie was eaten and good-bye said, Maggie and I left school together. Shouldering our carefully packed backpacks, we walked slowly, talking over plans. I unfolded the little slip of paper from my fortune cookie. "Be bold. Nothing is gained without risk." Fitting maybe, but I didn't know if I should be taking advice from a dessert.

P.L. had said he was staying at the Forest View Motel. It was almost on our way home. We made the detour. Then we headed toward the room with the parking lot's lone rental car out front.

He answered the door at our second knock, wearing a rumpled blue bathrobe over his clothes. He'd probably been trying to take a nap.

"We're sorry to disturb you," Maggie said in her most

polite, grown-up sounding voice. "But you said that if you could actually go to one of the worlds you write about, you'd do it."

"Sure. That's every writer's dream. But it's just that, a dream."

"It doesn't have to be. If you give us a chance, we'll show you how to make it real."

P.L. shrugged. "You're writing a fantasy story? Well, come in. At least you're something a little different." He ushered us in and sat on the edge of one of the twin beds. We sat on the other.

Feeling kind of stupid, I launched into an account of the blue aliens, their high-tech device, and their explanation about humans being "actualizers." Then I described what happened the last two times we'd used the gizmo.

When I'd finished, he said, "Kid, write that into a story and you're guaranteed to win the next contest."

I shook my head. "I know it sounds dumb, but it really is true. Look, here's the circlet and staff." I pulled them from my backpack. The silver circlet's three blue jewels and the short staff that plugged into them glowed in the motel lamplight.

"Intriguing," he commented, "but not particularly alien looking."

Then his eyes opened really wide. *"That* is, though." He pointed a shaking finger at the thing crawling out of my bag.

"Leggy!" I snapped. "I said you couldn't come." I glanced at P.L. He looked totally stunned and way more willing to believe. After all, a multi-legged, polka-dotted creature that's into mind reading is pretty convincingly alien.

I smiled at the author. "This is a dit-dit, the little guy who came back with us from Planet Yastol. I wouldn't let him come on the last trip we made, and he's still miffed."

Maggie grabbed a cold piece of toast from a room service tray. Leggy hopped onto the table and began happily shredding the bread. Maggie smiled. "Leggy's got really sharp teeth, but if he thinks you're a friend of Josh's, he won't do that to you."

P.L. gulped. "Right. Josh, you're my new best friend." Then he laughed. "Is that some sort of remote-controlled thing? You had me fooled for a moment."

I shook my head. "Nobody controls Leggy."

Maggie grabbed the circlet out of my hand and smiled

at the author. "Let's make a deal. You put this on and let us stick in the staff. If nothing happens, fine. We'll take Leggy and head back home. But if it works, hold out your hands so we can come along to Wyrd World with you."

He laughed. "Deal. On the condition that you let me use this idea in one of my next books. It's got potential."

"Deal," Maggie and I both said, smiling.

That was the last time any of us smiled for quite a while.

## CHAPTER TWO
# GETTING THERE

When we put the circlet on P.L., we told him to think of some place on Wyrd World. You'd think I would have known to be more specific!

As Maggie stuck the staff's prongs into the jewels, we all grabbed hands. There was an electric jolt and an awful inside-out feeling before we were swept away. When we staggered to a stop, P.L.'s look of astonishment was priceless. Quickly, it turned to a look of horror.

"Duck!" Maggie screamed.

I turned around and gasped. Leggy dove from my shoulder into my shirt. Maggie and I each grabbed one of P.L.'s arms and pulled the stunned author to the rocky ground. A feather-bedecked spear sailed over our heads.

"Oh no, oh no, oh no!" P.L. muttered.

"Oh yes," I muttered back. "This is your Wyrd World, all right. But why choose to land us in the middle of a battle?"

"I . . . I just thought about a scene I'm writing now, a small skirmish between rebels and the soldiers of Gaurgum."

"Gaurgum?" Maggie snorted. "You also had that dump in book three. Why couldn't you think of a *nice* scene, like the forest of Inj or the Fathian Isles?"

"All you said was . . ."

"It's all right," I assured him. The guy looked like he was about to cry. "Gaurgum is cool too. All we need to do is . . ."

"Hide!" Maggie hissed. "Soldiers coming this way!"

Peering over boulders, we saw guys in purple armor climbing toward us. "The Elite Guard," P.L. groaned. "We don't want to get caught by them. Try to hide down there." He pointed to a crevasse half hidden under a boulder. Trying to make ourselves flat as cockroaches, Maggie and I squeezed underneath. Before P.L. got in past his waist, he was yanked out.

"Got one!" a voice bellowed. Then it laughed. "One of their wizards, by the look of him."

*Right. The blue bathrobe,* I thought. *On Wyrd World, wizards wear blue.*

"No, no, I'm a writer, not a wizard!" he screamed. "And you shouldn't treat wizards like this anyway!" He kept it up all the way down the hill, describing the horrible spells he'd cast on them if he were a wizard.

Maggie and I struggled out of the crevasse and watched them march off toward the Fortress of Gaurgum. "Oh, great," Maggie sighed. "We've been on this world less than a minute, and already we've lost our school's famous author. Plus our only way home."

"Hey, this was *your* idea," I said.

"Okay. So now it's your turn to come up with an idea."

I groaned. "Follow them, get P.L. and the circlet back, and *never use that gizmo again!*"

We stood up and began creeping from boulder to boulder, keeping an eye on the soldier who'd thrown P.L. over his shoulder like a sack. The fortress they were heading for looked even grimmer than I'd imagined from reading the book. "A fearful fortress of darkness," P.L. had called it. Built in a long-extinct volcanic cone, it had a massive iron gate set in its base. That led to the great courtyard in the hollow interior. Rooms and stairways had been tunneled into the mountain walls. We couldn't see all that from where we were, of course, but having read the book helped.

"Okay, book three," Maggie said. "Gaurgum—what do we know about the place?"

"Thick walls, mean guards, dungeons, and . . ." I grinned, "a secret entrance."

"Right! What's-his-name, the renegade monk, used it to sneak in and sabotage the head guy's sacred divinator or whatever."

I nodded. "If we can sneak around to the back, we might be able to recognize the rocks that mark the secret entrance. Good thing I reread all those books when I heard P. L. Cuthbertson was coming."

The idea that the two of us (three if you count Leggy) could actually pull off a rescue was pretty farfetched. But at least the sneaking part might not be too hard. The sun was setting—P.L. had described it as "a gargantuan golden orb"—and the plain along the way to the fortress was splotched with boulder shadows.

"Finding the right markers for the hidden entrance might be harder after sundown," I whispered, "but light from the twelve moons should help."

We set off sneaking, and in the darkened sky, small moons started popping out like Ping-Pong balls. It was beginning to get cold, and I was glad I'd insisted we bring heavy jackets to school that day, on the off chance that Maggie and I followed through on her crazy idea.

Why do I let her talk me into these things?

We saw no other movement on the plain. Probably because Gaurgum's fortress dwellers close the gates at sunset. Maggie and I circled around to the back of the former volcano. From what P.L. had written, probably no one inside the fortress knew about this old secret entrance. That was good. Less good was the huge number of rocks piled all around the mountain base.

"Rock pillars are supposed to mark the spot, right?" Maggie muttered. "So which of the several hundred rock pillars would those be?"

I frowned, trying to remember. "He said something about the first one looking . . . 'almost good enough to eat.'"

"Great. Like that one that looks like a muffin? Or how about those gumdrop-shaped ones? Or that pair that look like corn on the cob?"

She was right. Use your imagination, and half of the rocks at ground level looked like cookies or hamburgers or bottles of soda. We trudged on and on. *How else had he described it?* I wondered. *Ah!*

I ran to one rock and hugged it like a long-lost friend. The pillar was tall and thin with natural grooves spiraling down it like stripes on a candy cane. Beyond it was the second marker rock, tall and squarish with grooves that looked like a giant cat had used it for a scratching post. And hidden behind that was a narrow cleft.

Maggie slid sideways through the tight passageway. I followed, trying not to bump Leggy, who seemed to be sleeping comfortably inside my shirt. I sighed with relief as my feet felt the promised flight of stairs. Definitely the right place.

The steps that climbed up the mountain were hidden from view by a wall of rock. They were open to the dim night sky and strewn with rubble like they hadn't been used for years. A real possibility, since the third Wyrd World book had been set sometime in the planet's past.

That last thought got me worrying. *Is this route still going to work after all those years?* I wondered. *Suppose a rockslide closed it off farther up. Or maybe someone sealed it off.*

I know, I know. I'm a born worrywart. Usually for good reason.

We'd been climbing so long that my legs wobbled and

my feet hurt from stumbling over loose rock. Suddenly Maggie squealed and fell back against me. "The path! It's gone!"

## CHAPTER THREE
# GOING IN

Grabbing at the rock wall to keep from tumbling down the stairs, I squinted past Maggie. In the dim light, I couldn't see a thing. Then I realized why. There was nothing to see. The path was gone.

I inched forward. A deep chasm dropped down before me into utter darkness. The slats of a rope bridge dangled down across from us, about twelve feet away on the far side.

"Great," Maggie said. "The bridge is out. Now what do we do?"

*Okay*, I thought. *Options: We can turn back and spend the rest of our lives hanging out in Wyrd World, while awful things happen to our visiting author. We can turn back and try to find another way into the fortress, a way that almost certainly doesn't exist. Or we can try to jump across the twelve-foot gap.*

I gave that last one a little more thought. Maggie did still have part of the alien gizmo with her.

"Maybe we could use the staff to pole-vault across," I said.

"What do you think we are, Olympic athletes?" Maggie replied.

Just then my chest itched frantically. Leggy shot out of my shirt and plunged into space.

"No!" Maggie and I both screamed, but he had already disappeared in the gloom.

Then we heard a cocky chirp. Looking across the drop, I saw a multi-legged shape clinging to the frayed end of the dangling rope bridge. Like a rocket, Leggy leaped back toward us. He landed on my head, trilling, as we scrambled to grab the rope he held.

"Thanks, Leggy," I managed to say. "That was incredible." Even with the translator net I picked up on Yastol, I could never pick up words from Leggy. But he started trilling in a smug way.

Looking at the bridge once we'd tied it tight on our end, I was feeling a lot less smug. Its ropes were frayed. Some of the planks were missing. But what choice did we have? Leggy scampered across first. Easy for him, he weighed next to nothing. Maggie crawled over on hands and knees, whimpering all the way. Okay, so I whimpered too when it was my turn. But not for long. Soon I started to scream.

A rope snapped behind me, and I clung to one plank as the bridge swung back and forth against the far wall of the rocky gap. Like a crazed monkey, I scrambled upward as bits of rope and wood broke off beneath me, clattering into the darkness below.

Near the top of the steps, my quivering legs didn't want to work, but somehow I stumbled on and on, up and up until . . . a blank rock wall. I sank to the ground, my spirits sinking even lower.

Staring at the wall, I slowly realized it wasn't quite blank. There were little rocky knobs all over it.

Maggie must have seen them too. "That's right! What's-his-name got through this wall somehow."

Maggie skims when she reads. I read carefully. "I remember now," I said. "He pressed a rocky knob and a secret panel opened up."

"Okay, smart guy, which of several of these thousand rocky knobs would that be?"

I may read carefully, but P.L. still doesn't always include every detail. But then, he never expected real people to be reading his story for how-to directions. We started punching and twisting the knobs.

After what seemed like ages, while I was in a knob-punching trance, the wall suddenly swung open. I fell flat on my face against a dusty stone floor. Good thing there was nobody in the room. In fact, there wasn't much of anything in the room, except a carpet of dust and curtains of cobwebs. *An unused storeroom,* I guessed. The only light was from milky moonbeams seeping past the doorway I'd fallen through. We used it to find a second door across the room, a wooden one, and slowly creak it open.

The next room was empty too, but it looked like it often wasn't. A table and benches ran along one wall. Another was lined with what looked like school lockers, only made of wood.

"So what's your plan?" Maggie whispered.

Plan? Ha. "Uh . . . find P.L. Maybe he's being questioned somewhere. Or maybe he's sitting in a dungeon. Or maybe he's . . ."

"Dead."

"No, he can't be!" I said. "I mean, they think he's a wizard. And wizards are important people in this world."

"But he can't do any magic!"

"Maybe they won't find that out. And he seems to be able to understand these people even without our translator nets, maybe because he's written so much about them. And he's got the blue robe and the circlet, so maybe . . ."

We heard voices. Coming our way. Frantically, we looked for some place to hide. I grabbed the handle of a locker door. Unlocked. I slipped in and Maggie took the next one.

". . . never learn, these rebels. One hopeless small-scale attack after another. What do they expect to gain?"

"To harass us, to wear us down," growled a second voice. "At least we caught one of their wizards this time. Good thing we hung a spell-queller outside his cell. He keeps threatening us with all kinds of evil. But once the commandant questions him, we'll learn their plans."

"When's the commandant expected back?"

"Tomorrow morning. Then we'll have some good times in the dungeon." What followed can only be described as an evil laugh.

Their footsteps came closer. I scrunched farther back into the crowded locker.

"That louse Burbek never returned my snakeskin vest. No, wait, that was Torill." A locker door rattled nearby.

"Well, grab it and let's go. Shift's almost over."

The footsteps trailed off and a door closed. I fought my way through some hanging clothes.

"Good idea," Maggie said, as I stepped out of the locker.

"Huh?"

"Disguising ourselves in clothes from these lockers."

"Right." I pulled the cloth off my head. It was a short cape made of scaly green skin. We rummaged in lockers until Maggie found a purple tunic and I added baggy yellow pants to my outfit.

I looked at my watch, but our time and this world's time were probably way different. "It sounds like we only have till morning to get to P.L."

"So where's the dungeon?" Maggie asked.

"Down."

"Duh. Any idea how to get there?"

"Find some stairs," I huffed. "Look, the book was a *story*. It didn't give a floor-by-floor plan of the fortress.

But I think the stairs are on one side of a big hall with lots of statues."

"What happens if someone stops us?"

"They won't," I said, without a clue whether I was right. "All we've got to do is act like we're going somewhere, delivering something maybe. Let's grab a couple of sacks, stuff them with some clothes and our jackets, and head out of here."

Carrying leather sacks bulging with wadded-up clothes, we timidly opened the locker room door. Taking a deep breath, I marched down a hallway. Torches set in the walls showed closed doors but very few people moving about. No one paid us much attention. Our clothes were no odder than anyone else's. Still, that didn't keep me from feeling like I had *intruder* written on me in neon letters.

Whenever we came upon stairs going downward, we took them. I was almost feeling confident until we rounded one corner and met a ten-foot-high guy with a sword. He stood stock still. So did we. Leggy peeked out from my shirt, squeaked, and ducked back in.

Maggie grunted and poked me. "Get moving," she whispered. "It's a *statue*."

"Umm, right. The hall of statues." We peeked out from under the stone guy's sword. The hall was larger than I'd imagined, but being lower down in the mountain's side, I guess there had been room for digging out a big, open space. Tall statues rested all around the sides, and here and there, groups of real people were talking to one another. Some of the statues were nonhuman and scary enough, but the people were scarier.

"I think we've got to head to the far side," I whispered. "But don't gawk like a tourist. Act like we work here every day."

That wasn't easy, since some of the statues really deserved gawking. Most had an uncommon number of arms and heads. We were almost across when a shout froze me mid-step.

"You there!"

## CHAPTER FOUR
# DEEP, DARK DUNGEON

I felt Leggy curling into a tight ball inside my shirt. Weighed with dread, I turned around. A large man with gold tassels on his red robe was talking with a soldier-looking guy. Tassel man gestured for us to come to him.

"Should we run?" Maggie whispered. "They look tougher, maybe faster than us."

We slunk toward them.

Tassel man thrust another leather sack at me, then turned back to his conversation. I peeked in and saw dirty clothes. *Right. We're a couple of laundry workers,* I thought. We scurried off.

At the far side of the hall were three doors. One was closed, one led to stairs going up, and one to stairs going down. We took the third one.

Down and down and down. Smoking torches gave off just enough light to keep us from tumbling.

"I sure hope this is right," Maggie muttered. "At least it's getting dank and cold."

She was right. The air and stones were starting to feel a lot like they're supposed to in dungeons. Finally, the stairs ended in a hallway going in two directions. As we thought about which way to turn, Leggy crawled out from my shirt, hopped down, and scuttled along the left-hand corridor. Shrugging, Maggie and I followed.

The rock walls were rougher than the ones upstairs, and the torches were farther apart. The hallway opened into a large low-ceilinged room that had five barred doorways set in its walls. A dungeon if I ever saw one. Which, actually, I hadn't.

The barred doors were all partly open. Except one.

That was the one with the big, burly guard sitting in front of it. Not a lot of doubt about where P.L. was. We shrank back into the shadows and whispered ideas.

"We could run out yelling, 'Fire! Everyone flee!'" Maggie suggested.

"Wouldn't he expect us to flee too?" I asked.

"Yeah, but maybe he'd unlock the door and drag his prisoner out. Then we could overcome him."

I grunted. "Have you noticed the great big sword in his lap?"

"So what's your bright idea?"

"We could walk up like we have something for him in these bags, and while he's opening them, we could hit him on the head with the staff."

"Have you noticed the great big helmet on his head?" Maggie replied.

Before we could come up with any more stupid ideas, Leggy squirmed out of my shirt, jumped down, and did something amazing. He swelled. The scales that usually lie flat along his back stuck up like porcupine quills. His whole body got bigger, like he was a balloon, eyes red and huge. And his polka dots began glowing. Our little dit-dit looked downright fearsome.

The guard seemed to think so too. As Leggy stalked forward, the big man jumped to his feet.

"What's that horrid thing?" he quavered, brandishing his sword. "Stay back!"

Ignoring the sword, Leggy growled and sprang forward, landing on the guard's chest. His feelers tore at the man's beard, then pinched his already large red nose.

With a shriek, the guard dropped his sword and rushed down the hallway. As soon as he disappeared, we charged to the unguarded door.

"P.L., you in there?" I called.

"Josh? Yes!"

"How do we open the door?" Maggie called.

"The key's hanging just outside," P.L. cried. "Hurry!"

Looking up, we saw the key dangling, but it was so high up I had to jump several times before I could grab it. When the door finally creaked open, our visiting author stumbled out. His blue bathrobe was dirty, and his grimy face needed a shave. But far worse, his head was bare.

Maggie gasped. "What happened to the circlet? We can't get home without it."

P.L. hung his shaggy head. "I'm sorry. I'm so sorry. They

took it. I thought it would help matters if they thought I really was a wizard. But they must have thought the circlet was something valuable and wizardly . . . because they took it to add it to the tribute they're about to send off to Mortalon. Gaurgum is a vassal of the Kingdom of Mortalon, you see. Vassal fortresses gain favor with King Torax the more tribute they send in."

"Right." P.L. sometimes wrote about Wyrd World's very complicated political system, but those were the parts even I rushed through.

"So how do we get it back?" Maggie squeaked. When her voice gets that high, I know she's scared. Maybe as scared as I felt.

"Find the tribute wagon or follow it to Mortalon," P.L. said. "This way!"

He headed toward a narrow doorway between two of the dungeon cells.

"Wait!" I said and looked around. Then I saw Leggy sitting nearby, casually scratching his side. He'd returned to his usual smaller and only slightly creepy self.

"Good work," I murmured. I felt a tinge of uneasiness as the amazing creature crawled up my arm. "I had no idea you could do that sort of thing." His only answer was a slight chirp as he curled up inside my shirt. I wondered just what else the dit-dit was capable of.

The passage P.L. led us through was narrow and lit only by scattered knobs of glow-in-the-dark rock. It also smelled. Smelled of . . .

"Oh no!" I suddenly remembered something from book two. "We're not going up one of those . . . chutes?"

"I'm sorry. So, so sorry. But it's the only way."

Maggie clutched my arm. "No way! Oh no. Please, *please*, no!"

## CHAPTER FIVE
# A SMELLY, BUMPY ESCAPE

The stink was getting really bad. It smelled like a gigantic sewer. For good reason. P.L. had written that the castles and fortresses of Wyrd World all had "sewage systems"—usually just chutes in the walls that emptied sinks, bathtubs, and toilets. And we had to climb up one of those chutes.

Standing by the incredibly stinky, gross-looking pit at the bottom, we could see rusty iron rungs leading up one wall. These were for the occasional sewer repair people. With more muttered apologies, P.L. started climbing. Maggie and I exchanged hopeless looks. Trying to squinch my nose closed, I followed. Whimpering, Maggie followed me.

Scattered splotches of glowing rock gave some light. So did light filtering through the toilet and sink openings above. Suddenly one of those lights blanked out. Someone had sat on a toilet.

I felt like screaming. Instead, I flattened myself to the wall as nastiness streamed by me. Below me, I heard Maggie gag. Then the light appeared again. The bare bottom was gone.

We kept climbing. Above that set of openings was another. "Maybe we shouldn't climb much higher," P.L. whispered down to me. "Josh, you're closest to that one. Swing over and pop your head out. See if anyone's around."

*Pop my head out?* Out of the toilet, he meant. *There had better not be anyone around*, I thought. *Or else we'll have a major freak-out—on everyone's part.*

I swung. I popped. Nobody was there. With great effort, I wriggled through the toilet hole.

It was kind of a nice, snug bathroom, with white tiles and all, but I wasn't there to admire the facilities. When the others joined me, we headed out the door.

Immediately our luck ran out.

"Who are you?" demanded a tall man dressed in white and gold.

"Eh . . . here for repairs," P.L. offered.

"We didn't ask for repairs."

"Just routine maintenance, that's all. Come along, crew."

The white-and-gold guy followed us with suspicious eyes. Obviously, he smelled something wrong besides our sewer-reeking clothes.

We hurried down the hallway and ran smack into a spear-toting guard.

"Stop them!" the man behind us called. "They're unauthorized here."

That's when we ran. Footsteps thundered behind us. "Halt!"

*No way*, I thought. Our hallway rounded a corner. Two sets of stairs lay ahead—one up, one down. P.L. took the upstairs route. I nearly tripped over a bucket and mop, then deliberately sent them clattering down the other stairs, hoping they would sound like us.

Our stairs ended in what looked like a laundry room. Sheets hung on a line, and just beyond them we heard voices.

I shrank back against a wall—and it gave way. Laundry chute!

I landed upside down on neat piles of clean laundry, rolling away just before Maggie and P.L. landed on top of me. We scrambled to our feet, bolted to a door, and looked outward at stone pavement lit by gray early-morning light. The great inner courtyard of the fortress.

Several people were nearby. Bad. And several wagons. Good. Hitched to the wagons were gudi, the long-legged lizards the Wyrd Worlders use like horses.

None of the Gaurgumites were looking our way. P.L. crouched down and crept toward the closest wagon. The guy's really pretty gutsy for a writer.

We lifted the loose canvas cover and slipped in among boxes and bags of stuff. "I'm guessing these are the tribute wagons being sent to Mortalon," P.L. whispered. "Maybe the circlet is here."

Careful not to shake the canvas cover, we started peeking into the bags and boxes. A crate of round, turquoise fruit. Bags of glass marbles. A case of copper spoons. Several boxes of books. A bale of furs from some shaggy yellow animal.

Suddenly the wagon jerked and began moving. We hunkered down among the cargo. One of the harnessed gudi screeched like a fire siren. Their normal noise, I think.

We rolled past the people working and talking in the courtyard. Behind us came the sounds of more wheels and gudi screeches. *The other wagon must be moving too,* I thought. Orders were shouted. Metal grated against metal. I prayed that we were getting out of the fortress and that the circlet was coming with us.

Our wagon was making enough noise for us to risk prying into a few more parcels. But we found no jewels or treasure, like you might expect a silver crown to be grouped with. Maybe it was in the other wagon. If not, we were in even deeper trouble.

We rocked and rolled on and on. After a while the rocking got to me. I fell asleep.

We must have traveled all day, because when Maggie poked me, the light filtering through the canvas was fading.

"Sounds like we've come to a town," she whispered.

I listened. It did sound like a town, minus the car horns, sirens, and squealing brakes. People were calling, yelling, and laughing. Two of them nearby started to argue.

"I don't care what you claim your cargo is, tribute or manure! Nothing enters the castle without inspection."

"Our cue to leave," P.L. whispered. I couldn't have agreed more. We slipped off the wagon, hoping to go unnoticed.

We didn't.

"Stowaways!" someone shouted. "Stop them!"

We ran, a husky wagon driver and an armored guard lunging after us. The street was crowded, but that helped. Dodging stray people and pushing through groups, we got farther and farther ahead. Soon we'd lost them—and gotten lost ourselves.

We stood panting in a trash-strewn alley. I had no idea where we were. P.L. hadn't written much about the back streets of Mortalon.

"What now?" Maggie asked.

P.L. shook his head. "If the circlet's in the castle, we need to get there too. But now's not the time, I think."

"So what time is it?" Maggie asked sulkily.

"Breakfast time."

That sounded better.

"But we don't have any local money," I pointed out.

P.L. shrugged. "There are so many different countries

and currencies on this world, people usually accept any coin that looks like silver."

We pooled our pocket change, then started looking for a tavern. We found a shabby little place with a sign showing a bowl and spoon swinging over the door. Inside, it had dirt floors and dirtier tables. When a waiter shambled over to us, we plunked down a dime and a quarter in exchange for a rock-hard loaf of bread and a sweaty lump of smelly cheese. I was hungry enough to eat but passed on the jug of frothy gray drink the tavern keeper had left.

When all that was left was crumbs, P.L. looked around and suddenly dropped his mug. "I can't believe it," he whispered. "It's Toraleen."

I half turned to see where he was looking. A slender woman sat hunched over a mug at the next table. A wisp of silver hair escaped from her green hood.

"Toraleen!" Maggie whispered excitedly. "Book two, *Queen of Rebels!* You sure it's her?"

P.L. nodded. "Crescent tattoo on her right cheek."

I stared, trying to look like I wasn't. *"A pale crescent tattoo on a bronzed cheek,"* I thought. *"A glint of ice-blue eyes."* *Toraleen, Alpha Spy of the Ty-Burazi!*

Just then the woman stood up, pulled her hood tighter, and headed for the door. P.L. followed. Maggie and I followed him.

When we got outside, Toraleen was striding down a narrow, busy street. She turned a corner and disappeared. We edged around a gudi-cart and an old woman selling withered fruit, getting to the corner in time to see Toraleen turning yet another one.

We sped after her, dodged around a potions cart, turned another corner, and . . .

"Yelp!"

P.L. staggered back. A thin, silver knife was held to his throat.

"Following me, are you?"

## CHAPTER SIX

# SHAKY ALLIANCE

You know the term *wicked grin*? Sounds corny, but that's exactly what was on the Alpha Spy's face.

Maggie ignored both the grin and the knife. "Yes, we are. Because you're Toraleen, and you're awesome!"

The woman turned on Maggie with a snarl.

"You know me?"

P.L. tried to answer, but the knife against his throat twitched, and he sputtered to a stop.

Quickly, I said, "Hey, don't hurt him. We're the good guys! And you are Toraleen, Alpha Spy of the Ty-Burazi. Your dad was Alpha Spy before you, until the Mortalon soldiers captured and executed him, and . . ."

Maggie interrupted. "And you had to beat out Arthat the Arrogant for the job, which made you really happy because you two had been rivals since you were kids. You're awesome at archery and hand-to-hand combat, but you worry about your spear-throwing skill and . . ."

"Halt! How do you know all this?" Toraleen's eyes were wide and almost frightened. She looked at P.L. more carefully, taking in his less-than-clean but still blue bathrobe. Slowly, she lowered her knife.

"The prophesy," she whispered. "Are you the Blue Seer spoken of in legend, whose coming foretells great change?"

"Oh no," Maggie said. "He's just . . ."

P.L. coughed. The author had a surprising gleam in his eyes. "Er . . . I might be. I . . . eh . . . do know things. And so do my assistants. But one of our . . . eh . . . implements of power was taken as tribute to Mortalon's king. And we must get it back. We could use your help in that regard, honored lady."

Toraleen sheathed her knife. "Indeed I will help you, Great Blue Seer. I too have an interest in 'freeing' Mortalon's ill-gotten tribute. For days, I have been watching tribute wagons entering the castle. The trick is in getting the tribute out again."

I frowned, remembering something from book three. Or was it five? Either way, there was another bad-guy castle that had been broken into. That was halfway across Wyrd World from where we were. But a group of rebels had managed it.

"How about getting help from the Ouliths?" I suggested.

"Or the Murmazites," Maggie said.

P.L. nodded. "Or the Chezoptrans might be useful."

Toraleen stared at us. "True, all those people have reason to hate the Mortalon. But my people have . . . little love for them."

"That's your problem here," P.L. complained. "You all never get your act together! Lots of folks hate being trampled on by the Mortalon or the other petty empires on this world, but you never unite against them. If you did, you could weaken, even overthrow them."

She stared at us a long time, her mouth open showing sharp, pointed teeth. "That would be a change indeed, as the prophesy promised. A difficult change. But, yes, perhaps we could approach the Ouliths. There is a colony near here."

P.L. nodded. "Deep in the Thanoi Valley, where they were driven by Mortalon raids."

Toraleen guided us through a maze of alleys and tunnels to one of the safe houses where a supporter let her stay in the attic. As we hunched under the low roof, the Alpha Spy and Blue Seer talked strategy. I was a little worried about P.L.'s trying to pass himself off as a wizard. But he seemed a lot happier than he had at the school.

Maggie and I tried to help with the plotting, but soon we were fast asleep on a pile of straw. It had been a long and very strange night and morning.

I woke once to find P.L. snoring beside me (news flash: famous authors snore) and Toraleen watching over us like a mother cat. I felt kind of guilty that we were letting her think we were magic workers—but not so guilty that it kept me awake.

I woke again to moonlight slanting through the tiny

attic window. Toraleen reverently poked at P.L., who woke with a snort so loud that Maggie jolted awake too.

Toraleen had found us three dark, hooded capes to hide our lighter clothes. She'd also come up with a pouch of food and gave us thick biscuit-things that tasted like slightly sweetened sawdust. Then we were out of the attic again, sneaking through the back alleys of the town.

As we hurried along, I thought about the Ouliths. They had been fun to read about. They'd starred in a couple of chapters in *Woe of the Wyrd Woods*. But did I really want to meet any in the flesh—or in the slime?

It took that night and most of the next day to get to the Oulith colony. Once outside the city, we walked through farmland that became swampier and swampier until we were hopping from one grassy ridge to another. The few trees around sagged with moss. The swampland finally plunged into a deep valley, with moss falling in curtains across rock walls. We couldn't see more than a few feet ahead of us because of the valley's thick, clammy mists.

It was downright creepy. And suddenly dangerous. Spears thunked into the muck all around us.

One moment the swamp had seemed lifeless. The next, we were surrounded by Ouliths. Ouliths may be the grossest creatures you could imagine: six-foot-long, puke-colored slugs. They have three sets of arms along their sides and lots of feet underneath. Lots and lots of feet. That makes them way faster than slugs. Ouliths also have gooey feelers on their heads, the way Earth slugs do, only the Ouliths have about ten each. The feelers wiggle when they talk. Or in this case, shout.

"Halt strangers! Explain your presence or die!"

Not too friendly, these guys.

Toraleen held both hands out, palms forward. "Greetings, mighty Ouliths. We come in peace."

"Then you can very well *go* in peace. And quickly!"

She seemed undaunted. "We cannot go until we explain why we came. We seek an alliance."

I think the mass barfing sound was a huge group laugh. "An alliance? With your sort? Such a thing is unheard of."

Toraleen swirled the dark cape off P.L., revealing his (even-more-stained) blue bathrobe. "But here is something of which you *have* heard. The legendary Blue Seer walks among us. His arrival heralds a time of change.

A time of weakening for this world's tyrants and of strengthening for their enemies. For all of us."

You'd think that the sight of a scrawny bespectacled author in a dirty blue bathrobe would set off another round of barfing laughter. But instead, there were gasps. All the Ouliths slid closer, wiggling their feelers.

The lead slug slid closest of all, dribbling slime at our feet. "But how do we know he is truly the Blue Seer?"

"He knows things," Toraleen answered. "Tell them something, Great One. Something they might think secret."

For a moment, P.L. just stood staring at the creatures he thought he'd created. No words came to him. I'd read the Wyrd World books more recently than P.L. had written them. So I whispered, "Tell them about the sacred cave that only Ouliths may enter."

"Right." P.L. crossed his arms and stared at the spokes-slug. "You have, at the northernmost end of this swamp, a sacred cave where young Ouliths go to learn the ways of their kind. In the center lies a pool of ever-bubbling mud, over which youngsters must spring across to prove their courage. Though at times, some jumpers have cheated by protecting their feet with boots of wax."

"You cannot know this!" the spokes-slug shouted.

P.L. grinned and continued. "Once, your great leader Burlagoog was proven to have cheated in this way when he was a youngster. This caused a great scandal, and he had to forfeit his right to the First Fruit Tasting."

A great howl rose up. Spears were shaken angrily, and a great shower of them rained down around us, trapping us in a tight little cage.

Perhaps that hadn't been the wisest secret to reveal.

## CHAPTER SEVEN

# GATHERING FORCES

"Rash ones!" Toraleen shouted from our spear-walled cage. "Naturally, a seer knows secrets both good and shameful. His knowing them is proof of his greatness. Listen to us, or risk being left in the dust of history!"

I cringed. *Should she be talking that tough to bad-tempered slugs with lots of spears?* I wondered.

But the lead slug burbled a quiet, "Speak."

Toraleen nudged P.L. He looked like he was going to pass out. Sure, he was used to speaking in front of school kids, but not to a crowd of angry giant slugs. Still, he cleared his throat. "It is the same all over your world," he began. "The reason tyrants conquer and kill you, force you to pay huge tributes and work as their slaves, is that you do not unite. You will never overcome the Mortalonians and their like unless you join with the other peoples they have oppressed."

At that point, he seemed to run out of words. "Sure, it'll be hard," I added. "But it can start with little things, like . . . helping us get back an important magic object that Mortalon stole."

Maggie joined in. "It is a magical crown, and if the Mortalonians use it, they might be able to see things that you don't want them to see."

That wasn't exactly true, but it seemed to work. The slugs slurped and gulped among themselves until the lead one said, "All right. I and my generals will speak to you about a *short-term alliance*. Come. Let us drink athl together and make plans."

Athl turned out to be a muddy yellow soup scooped into clay cups from wooden troughs. It looked ghastly and tasted worse than it looked. The smell was enough to curl your toes. We three humans sipped ours. Toraleen took several brave swallows. The Ouliths gulped theirs down by the cupful.

The peacemaking was done under a canopy of gray-green moss that hung in curtains from drooping trees. Baby slugs only a foot long peeped through the moss and giggled like boiling teakettles. Maggie and I watched as some of the young slid and did tricks around the gnarled tree trunks.

The plans Toraleen and the Ouliths worked out sounded kind of complicated. They seemed to involve recruiting some other creatures named the Ijapati to help break into the Mortalon castle.

When the big slugs had gone off to arrange sleeping quarters for us, I asked P.L. about the Ijapati. I didn't remember reading about them.

"I mentioned them in the first draft of book four," he said, "but my editor had me cut that part out because they didn't figure in the story again. They're shy creatures. They can fly too. Most importantly, they don't totally hate the Ouliths."

Our dinner that night doesn't bear talking about. So I won't. Except to say "Blech!" We slept in hammock-things made from moss and stitched together with slime.

Leggy, who'd been hiding out since seeing his first Oulith, slept inside my shirt. In the morning, we couldn't face more Oulith food, so we breakfasted on some of Toraleen's dry rations. The biscuits suddenly tasted a whole lot better.

Then we set out. I'd imagined we'd go off with a whole army of fast, sliding slugs, but only five of them were with us. One was a half-grown slug, only three feet long. His name was something like Oooloop. He traveled in the rear with Maggie and me while the grown-ups walked ahead, talking strategy. Oooloop moved like a dog walking off-leash. He kept zipping back and forth along the path.

"Watch this!" he said for the umpteenth time, as he spiraled up a dead tree and flipped onto a rock ledge. "And this!" He sped along the ledge, swooped down a slope, and looped into a perfect landing in front of us. *What a major show-off*, I thought. But I was a little envious of the tricks he could do on his many little legs. Tricks I could never match on a skateboard.

After a while, the ground we covered became rocky. Ravines cut through the land ahead. The Ouliths kept grumbling that we two-legged types were so slow.

Finally, they made each of us ride on the back of an adult slug. Slugback riding is every bit as gross as it sounds. But it *was* faster.

Soon the bare rocks gave way to a forest of tall trees. The trunks were as straight as telephone poles. Spiky blue leaves stuck out all the way up. In a thicket of these trees, the slugs bucked us off. We found ourselves sitting on the needle-strewn ground looking up—up at eyes. Not slug eyes, either. Enormous purple eyes.

The Ijapati skittered down from the trees and circled around us. They had long, thin bodies with wispy gray hair covering them from top to bottom. Underneath their hairy arms, I could make out pairs of wings.

"They look like a pencil sketch of flying lemurs," Maggie whispered. "With pointy wings."

A weird description but kind of right. Although the creatures' big eyes would have to be done with a purple marker. One of the creatures inched forward, blinking rapidly, and said, "Go away!"

Another friendly bunch. But at least they didn't have spears.

Knives, yes.

The winged creatures waved their blades around until Toraleen stood up, made peaceful gestures with her hands, and launched into the talk about the Blue Seer prophesy. About how people could defeat bullies by uniting. Once again, it worked. I was happier than ever that P.L.'s bathrobe happened to be blue. And he seemed to be really getting into the part.  He wasn't tired or cranky anymore, even after his stay in the Gaurgum dungeon. A pair of half-grown Ijapati curled up at his feet, purring like adoring cats. At least the creatures' kids seemed nice.

This time the peacemaking-strategy meeting took place around cups of something that tasted like a mixture of cough syrup and steak sauce. Nasty, but I've had worse. I'd even had worse the day before.

That night we slept in bunks carved into the trunks of the spiky branchless trees. The next morning, a large party of Ijapati set out with us. The four two-leggers in our party rode slugback again. Once we left the odd blue forest, we crossed a dry, rocky wasteland, trudging toward a forest with more normal-looking trees. At the far edge of that forest, we were able to look out and see the distant city of Mortalon.

That's where most of our escort left us. Our party was down to P.L., Maggie and me, Toraleen, Oooloop, and the two young Ijapati we'd met earlier, sisters named Reesh and Roosh. They still purred a lot. I was surprised at the small size of our force, but Toraleen insisted we needed stealth, not numbers. Still, I would have felt safer with a blockbuster-movie-type massive army.

With our slug and stringy lemur companions, we obviously couldn't go straight through the town that sprawled beneath from the castle. So when dusk set in, we crept through scrubby grasslands toward the other side of the castle. The light of multiple moons revealed high castle walls perched on a cliff, surrounded by a moat full of dark, greasy water. I imagined all sorts of moat monsters lurking under the surface. No way did I want to swim across that.

At the edge of the moat, Oooloop kicked a dirt clod into the water. Something black arched up, gulped down the clod, and disappeared amid the inky ripples. *Nope*, I thought. *No swimming.*

Reesh and Roosh giggled together, then took to the air until they blended with the scattered clouds above. They trailed long ropes behind them. The plan was to tie the ropes to the castle's top battlements and climb up, P.L. explained. That didn't sound a whole lot better than swimming across the moat.

I was worried that we'd be easy for guards to spot once we got to the castle walls. But staring closely at Mortalon, I didn't even see anyone on patrol. Maybe King Torax figured no one would be able to unite against them. That Mortalon was safe from attack.

Soon there were five ropes dangling above our side of the moat. For a moment, I feared we'd have to swing across the water like Tarzans. But Oooloop had brought along slings—made, I suspected, from woven slug slime. He attached them to the bottoms of the ropes. We sat in the slings, trying not to freak out at the sliminess, as the two Ijapati carried us across the moat. It astonished me how strong those wispy-looking creatures were. They were quiet as wisps of smoke too. No more purring.

One by one, we crawled through an unlit castle window, and we were in! Piece of cake, this assault on the castle. Not one problem.

Not until a baby started wailing.

## CHAPTER EIGHT

# ROYAL WELCOME

Great. Betrayed by a squalling baby! My chest itched, and Leggy squirmed out and began scurrying toward the crib. I tried to grab him, but he hopped away and landed on the child's chest. *Not a good public relations move to let a royal child get shredded*, I thought.

I blinked. The kid's night lamp showed Leggy juggling toys from the crib. Colorful balls swirled through the air. The child stared at them with wide-eyed wonder, gurgling happily.

The rest of us tiptoed past the baby and its new babysitter and crept out a door. The hallway beyond was dimly lit and empty. But I still didn't think much of our chances of success. Sure, it was late at night and most people would be sleeping. Even so, there were sure to be guards somewhere or people getting up to go to the bathroom.

Toraleen had a hunch about where Mortalon's tribute would be stored, so we followed her down a spiral staircase and into another hall. A man in a nightshirt grinded to a halt in front of us. He raised his candle and stared before opening his mouth to yell. No sound got out. Oooloop reared up and shot off a wad of sticky stuff onto the man's face. Soon the poor guy was wrapped in bands of slime and stuffed under a bench.

"Wow," I whispered to Maggie. "When it comes to cool superpowers, shooting slug slime is now near the top of my list!"

Toraleen led us right to the Mortalon Treasury and proved herself a wonder at lock picking. Within seconds we were inside. "Treasury" was right— the room was full of treasure. It was stacked on tables, piled on shelves, and heaped on the floor.

Toraleen set about filling her pockets and a big bag with jewels and silver. It was kind of tempting to do the same, but Maggie, P.L., and I were only interested in one item. We searched everywhere, wading through jewelry, climbing up stacks of rare books, riffling through piles of silk. No luck. No circlet.

In fact, our luck had run out altogether. It must have been the avalanche of golden goblets that fell after P.L. pulled a gold crown from the bottom of the stack that alerted the forces of Mortalon. In moments, the treasury door flew open and two guards leveled their spears at us.

Well, not *all* of us. The Ijapati sisters, Reesh and Roosh, had shot up to the ceiling. Oooloop had slid under a low table. But Toraleen, Maggie, P.L., and I were truly trapped. I was really getting tired of people pointing spears at me.

I held up a silk pillow from the treasure pile, using it like a shield. Soon feathers were flying everywhere from its spear-slashed side. Toraleen was disarmed and I was too. Big hero. I almost urged Maggie to hit a guard with the staff, but I realized they might have confiscated it too. We were already defeated—it was smarter to keep the staff hidden.

This time there were four of us in a dungeon. The slug and the flying lemurs were still loose, but they didn't seem like the types to organize a jailbreak. And anyway, there must have been a dozen guards outside our cell.

At least we didn't have long to rot in the dungeon. By midmorning we were hauled out and marched to a throne room. It was chock-full of fancily dressed, chattering people. I guess we were the best entertainment they'd had in a while. But P.L., Maggie, and I didn't seem to be the featured attraction. It was Toraleen, Alpha Spy of the Ty-Burazi, that they were all excited about. She stood with us inside a ring of guards, looking unbothered by all the jeers thrown her way.

The crowd quieted down as two great golden doors were thrown open. A man and a woman strode in and sat themselves on raised thrones. Everyone bowed but us. It wasn't that I wanted to be rude. I was too busy staring.

"Her crown!" Maggie gasped. "She's got our circlet!"

She did. Jithia, queen of Mortalon, was proudly wearing the alien gizmo. It must have looked like a prime royal find when it came in on the tribute wagon. It even looked good on her, the circlet's silver glowing atop what our author had called "midnight-black tresses."

Without it, though, we'd be stuck on Wyrd World for the rest of our lives.

But then, as captured treasure thieves, that probably wouldn't be very long.

A fat soldier dripping with medals bowed to the royal couple, then straightened up and said, "Your Majesties, due to the vigilance of the guards under my command, Toraleen, the hated Alpha Spy of the Ty-Burazi, has been captured. With her are accomplices in her fiendish plan to steal your well-deserved tribute." As proof, he showed the bulging sack of jewels that Toraleen had been collecting.

"Hang her! Hang them!" shouted the crowd. I wished I had never read a piece of fiction in my life.

King Torax stood and the crowd quieted. "Hanging, yes. That is only right for such a notorious villain. But first, torture, I think. She is sure to have valuable information to extract."

The crowd clapped and cheered.

"What sort of sham trial is this?" Toraleen shouted above the din. "Have we no chance to make a statement?"

"No, you do not!" the king bellowed. "What is more . . ."

We never learned what more there was. Just then, an old woman burst into the throne room holding a big basket. She was sobbing miserably.

"Majesties, what am I to do?" she wailed. "A horrible creature has crawled into the little prince's bassinet. When I try to remove the foul thing, it hisses and snaps. I fear it will do harm to His Little Highness."

I craned to look. There was polka-dotted Leggy, snuggled up beside a baby. His Little Highness was chuckling and playing with one of the dit-dit's feelers.

The king and the queen hurried down from their thrones and bent over the basket. "Oh, horrible, *horrible!*" wailed the queen. The king timidly reached down, and Leggy immediately snapped at his royal fingers.

The king jumped back, and I jumped up. "Majesties! I recognize the creature. It's a rare and deadly dit-dit. I know how to remove it safely. In return, I ask only that you hand me the new crown that rests on the head of the queen."

"Impudent brat!" King Torax bellowed. "You will remove that creature now, or you will suffer greatly! A king does not bargain with thieves."

I answered the king, but I looked directly at Leggy.

"But your people stole it from us! I need it and *we cannot leave here without it!*"

Leggy got the message. He sprang out of the basket, snatched the circlet off the queen's head, and scampered toward us. Instantly, guards lunged at him. The dit-dit swerved to avoid them. Members of the court got into the act, trying to tackle Leggy and herd him away from me, Maggie, and Toraleen.

Two beefy guys had almost caught him when a fast-gliding slug knocked their feet out from under them. Leggy leaped over the head of another pursuer, and a pair of flying gray dust balls snatched him in midair. Reesh, Roosh, and Oooloop swerved toward us as people flung themselves out of the way. The little Oulith knocked aside our ring of guards, Reesh and Roosh landed on top of us, and Leggy jumped into my arms. I grabbed the circlet and jammed it on P.L.'s head. Maggie whipped out the short staff and stuck it in.

"Now, get us out of here!" I yelled over the royal hubbub.

"Right!" P.L.'s frightened eyes closed in concentration. My insides churned and stretched. A searing tornado seemed to race through my bones. Then screams rang out.

I took a peek between my fingers and saw hot darkness lit by red flares.

Struggling to disentangle ourselves, our crew stood up and looked around.

"Oh no!" P.L. wailed. "I'm sorry. So, so, sorry!"

## CHAPTER NINE
# THE MINES

P.L. was practically sobbing. "All I could think was that the Mortalon throne room was the worst place to be on this whole world—except for . . . for . . ."

"The mines of Karfax," Maggie finished for him.

"Yes," he whimpered, "where Mortalon sends captured subjects to toil until they die."

When I'd read that book, *Depths of Darkness*, I'd thought the mines of Karfax sounded awesome. The area wasn't a tunnel-type mine like we have on Earth. It was a giant, cone-shaped cavern with level after level of openings carved into its sides. Colored gems sparkled in its stone walls. Gems that slaves were forced to dig out.

Toraleen yelped in alarm. "Karfax! You moved us with your magic, Great Seer! Now move us on again. Quickly!"

Shaking and pale, P.L. closed his eyes for another try. Maggie had already removed the staff from the circlet, but she tried to stick it back in. Not quickly enough.

"Ho, escapees!" a voice boomed. A large gloved hand grabbed Maggie and lifted her up like a doll. "Get them all!"

A squad of soldiers burst out of a tunnel and attacked. We all fought, some more effectively than others. Toraleen kicked and punched several soldiers before they wrapped her in ropes. One soldier hoisted her over his shoulder. Another did the same with Maggie.

"Humanoid females," the lead soldier said. "Take them to level nine."

That was the last I saw of Maggie before the others and I failed to fight off more ropes.

"Take the Oulith to level seven," the head soldier barked, "and the Ijapati to level three. I'll take the humanoid males to level four. Someone's going to pay for letting this lot escape."

P.L. and I were bound like flies in spiderwebs. A couple of soldiers trundled Roosh, Reesh, and Ooolog down different tunnels. Then a soldier grabbed me too.

I hung upside down, my head banging against armor plating. But my brain hurt even more from an overload of weirdness. After almost being executed on an alien planet, my favorite author and I were being hauled off to slave for the rest of our lives in an alien mine. *Enough adventure!* I thought. *I really, really want to go home.*

The circlet, firmly crammed onto P.L.'s head, bounced along beside me. But the staff was headed to level nine with Maggie, wherever that was.

Finally, our corridor widened into a room. The soldier dumped us in a heap on the rocky floor. He chained iron cuffs to our ankles and locked them with a glowing red clamp. Then he spat and stomped off, probably to find someone to yell at for letting prisoners escape. If only we *could* escape. But that seemed as impossible as, well, as our whole situation.

I glanced at P.L., expecting to see him looking as miserable and hopeless as I felt. But instead, an intense gleam shone behind his thick glasses. He almost seemed to be smiling.

"I can't believe it," he muttered. "But I've got to. It's happening."

"Huh?"

"The reason I was thinking about this place, instead of someplace safer, must be because at home I'd been trying to plot out my next Wyrd World book. I'd decided to have my hero captured and sent to work in the Mortalon mines. I hadn't decided quite who my hero would be, but I was thinking he'd be a wizard . . . seized along with some of his apprentices and friends."

"Oh." The idea was sort of mind-thumping. "So you were almost predicting the future," I said. "The now-future, the here-future, when you just thought you were making things up."

"Yes! That must be it! But . . . I had to stop plotting the story so I could go off and talk to your school."

I felt the tiniest jab of hope. "Do you know how the heroes escape?"

P.L. frowned. "I hadn't quite solved that problem. Mostly, I was thinking about how different parts of the story could fit together—the wizard's wand, the sphere of power that runs all the Karfax mining equipment."

"And?"

"And I realized I could have him use the wand to destroy the sphere. But then I decided that one of the apprentices should really do it, since I wanted to make that kid the hero in my *next* book."

"Oh." Wyrd World was really living up to its name.

Just then, a guard even bigger and meaner-looking than the last one stomped toward us. He grabbed our chains and yanked us after him. Soon we were at the edge of a shallow pit. It was full of miserable folks scraping at the rock with picks. Some looked kind of human. Others were from different groups P.L. had mentioned in his stories: creatures with giant butterflylike wings or that looked like a cross between a giraffe and a crab. There were even a couple of Oulith slugs, though they had ropes wrapped around them so they couldn't slide away on their little feet. The whole lot looked banged up, underfed, and hopeless.

Our guard thrust a couple of picks into our hands and kicked us toward a patch of rocky wall. "Dig. If you break any gems or pocket any or slack off, you'll get a whipping you'll never forget."

To make his point, he wheeled around and slashed a whip across the miner next to us, a little sheeplike creature with six legs. It bleated in pain and redoubled its efforts to pick at the hard rock.

The guard stood back and watched as P.L. and I tried to use our picks like we knew what we were doing. Rock chips stung my face, grit clogged my throat, and I didn't see anything that looked like a gem. I heard a snap like a firecracker, and the guard's whip stung the back of my neck. I yelped and picked harder. The guard gave both me and P.L. parting kicks and sauntered away.

"P.L.," I whispered, "if your new book idea was sort of a prediction . . . could it really work? I mean, you're not really a wizard. We don't even have a wand."

"But I have this." P.L. reached into the pants pocket underneath his bathrobe and pulled out the little laser pointer he used in his school talk. "And I have you."

"Hey, I'm no wizard apprentice. And I don't know where any sphere of power is."

"But I might. The wizard I was creating—or thought I was creating—did. This is all very confusing. Anyway, see those lights?"

He pointed to a line of glowing red balls along the cavern walls. I hadn't really noticed them before, but they sure were different from the torches that had lit the castle. I nodded.

"They're powered by the magic sphere. So are the locks on the gates and on all the prisoners' chains. The Guild of Dark Wizards is allied with the kingdom of Mortalon. These evil wizards help run their mines. I was thinking that if my wizard's apprentice could steal the sphere of power, then . . ."

"Hold on a sec. That all might sound good in a book, but this is *real*, and these are real iron chains we're locked to."

At the sound of footsteps, we started picking furiously. When it was safe to talk again, P.L. was frowning. "I know, but I had decided that what I needed was some creature around them that could change its size—whose bite would make others change *their* size and slip out of their chains. I was playing with the idea of a pet bumblebee, but . . ."

He pointed to my right. Leggy had quietly slipped out from my shirt. The dit-dit sat watching us, his many legs crossed and a smug smile on his face.

"Oh come on. I mean, we did see Leggy swell up and get bigger. But what makes you think he can make others change size?"

P.L. shook his head. "That was the situation I thought I was creating. But if I'm not *creating* it, then maybe it actually exists here. Maybe your little friend has powers you don't know about . . ."

He nodded at Leggy. The did-dit grinned toothily. Suddenly he leaped at me and sunk his sharp teeth into

my ankle. I'd thought the whip had stung, but that was nothing. This hurt like fire had been shot into my veins. It also didn't feel so great when those veins—along with my bones and skin—started shrinking. It felt like I were being sucked into a vacuum from the inside outward.

Once I stopped shaking, though, I saw that the iron ankle clamp was much roomier—and that it came up to my waist. I clambered out of it. At least my clothes had shrunk too. It was cold in that mine.

"It worked!" P.L. exclaimed. He towered over me, looking like a crazed giant. "Amazing! I'd only been playing with ideas."

"Well, this *playing* isn't much fun," I squeaked up at him. "What do I do now?"

"Go! Steal the sphere of power. I'd pictured it in a dome at the top of this cavern. See the red glow way up there?"

He pointed out through an opening in our cave wall toward a great open space. High above the Karfax mines was a glowing red dot, like a rat's evil eye.

"Yeah, but I'm now just a few inches high," I said. "It'll take me ages to get up there."

"Not on your trusty steed it won't."

P.L. pointed a giant finger at Leggy. The little did-dit was now a *big* dit-dit—to me, anyway. Standing beside me, he was the size of a horse. The kind of horse who could reach out multiple legs and flip me onto its back. I clutched his raised scales.

"Okay, so if I can get to this sphere, what do I do?"

The author shrugged. "Well . . . I hadn't worked that out yet."

We heard a whip crack and a squeal of pain from farther along the cavern.

"Hurry!" P. L. said, then smiled sheepishly and handed me his laser pointer like it were a big sword. "Cheer up. My books usually end well for the hero."

"Yeah," I grumbled. "That's if you're writing *them*. What if *they're* writing *themselves*?"

## CHAPTER TEN
# THE STUFF OF HEROES

I didn't have much more time to talk about the mysteries of fiction. I was busy just holding on. Leggy charged off, though I doubted he had any better idea where we were going than I did. Just up.

In a long string of weird scary stuff, the trip toward the red dot was perhaps the weirdest and scariest. Leggy and I

95

were too low to the ground for most of the towering guards to notice us, though we did startle a few of the shorter prisoners. But we had to dodge a lot of feet and heavy carts wheeling back and forth with loads of rock. We took stairways or ramps when we found them, but sometimes we had to scramble straight up walls. Well, Leggy did the scrambling. I just clung on and kept my eyes shut.

Close to the top, there were no more hollowed-out levels with miserable chained prisoners. The stairways got narrower and steeper. And there were fewer guards about, though we did see some people who just might be wizards. Not that I should know what a wizard looks like. One was fat and bald; one was skinny and bushy-headed; and another was a short, freckled redhead. But they all wore blue. They had long capes, odd-looking jewelry, and sort of an electric feeling about them.

When we had almost reached the top, the redheaded one saw us. "Vermin!" he cried, waving a cane at us. It must have been some sort of magic wand, because it shot out a stream of fire. Leggy dodged it like a charging running back. Suddenly all three were after us, but the space in the stairwell became too narrow, and their own robes caught fire in the streams of flame.

With much cursing, the smoldering wizards kept after us. We scrambled on, then screeched to a halt at an arched window. Ahead of us hung the glowing red sphere. Below us, the cavern dropped away through many, many levels of emptiness.

"Stop them!" a wizard cried. "I smell power about them!"

I probably did smell after days of not bathing, but the only power I had was P.L.'s silly laser pointer. Yanking it out, I pointed it at our pursuers. They flinched back, maybe thinking it was a real magic wand. Then, when nothing happened, they surged forward again.

Leggy crouched down and took a leap. We soared toward the orange-sized sphere. As we splattered against it, Leggy grabbed hold of it with a bunch of legs. The glowing ball swung back and forth on the end of a silver chain. Not great. We were supposed to take the thing away, not swing on it like an amusement park ride. But even with the wild swinging, the chain didn't come loose.

Crowding at the arched window, the three wizards raised their wands. But they must have been afraid to fire and maybe hit the sphere. I slashed my laser light toward them and watched them duck. Then I shined it back and forth across the silver chain. Stupid, really— it was just a light. But teachers always warn that those things can hurt your eyes, and who knows what the chain was made of, anyway. Maybe something that didn't like laser light. Or maybe it was just our sudden weight change. With a painful fizzing noise, I stretched back to my original size.

The chain snapped. All the lights in the cavern, except our sphere, went out. We were falling, a long way down. Long enough for me to wonder how Maggie would explain to our folks that I'd died on a planet that most people thought existed only in books.

Down and down and . . . snatch! Something caught us. Reesh or Roosh! Whichever one it was purred happily.

The great cavern was dark without the sphere's energy. But not quiet. The prisoners' locks had opened, and everyone was running around, yelling and bumping into one another.

Reesh (or Roosh) carried us around the main cavern and flew alongside Roosh (or Reesh). Together they managed to find P.L., who was comforting our fellow prisoner, the frightened six-legged sheep. We found that if we touched the sphere to one of the dead globes on the rocky ceiling, the globe lit up again. One by one we lit more globes and eventually found Oooloop. Then we headed to level nine and retrieved Toraleen and Maggie.

Okay, I admit it. I hugged my sister. I was really glad to see her—and glad she didn't have to explain my mysterious death to our parents.

Finally, we were all in the same place again: Maggie, me, Leggy, Toraleen, Reesh, Roosh, Oooloop, and our visiting author. And we had both parts of the alien gizmo too.

"Well, I suppose we can leave now," P.L. said with a touch of sadness. Everyone nodded.

Maggie and I looked at each other. *We've come this far*, I thought. *Done this much.* "Maybe we should try a little something else first," I suggested.

P.L. smiled. So did Toraleen. Leggy crawled onto my shoulder, and I handed the Alpha Spy the sphere of power. She raised it above her head and shouted into the vast center of the cavern.

"All of you, former prisoners! You are unchained, thanks to the magic of the Blue Seer of Prophesy and his apprentices. But you will not be truly free until the tyrants of this world are overthrown. Tie up your guards and gather here. Let us take a moment to plan for the future."

Excited whisperings filled the vast space. Toraleen continued. "Before you return to your homes, let us forge an alliance. A united army of rebels who will act together to free our world from its oppressors. Come, let us gather to thank the wizards who freed us. And then let us bring about the change their coming foretold!"

Reesh—or was it Roosh?—flew about with the glowing sphere, lighting enough globes for the freed prisoners to find their way to the big open gallery where Toraleen gathered us. Most of the guards were quickly bound if they hadn't already fled. I chuckled, suspecting the three wizards had fled as well, in the face of our obviously superior magic.

At the gathering, there was a lot of grand talk about magic and prophesies. P.L., though his bathrobe's blue was almost totally coated with rock dust, played his part to the hilt. He looked a lot more comfortable than when he'd been talking to an auditorium full of school kids.

Maggie and I felt kind of silly playing the part of apprentice wizards. But we were happy too. Though we'd first met it in books, this world was real. And maybe we'd had a little part in making it better.

As the talking ended, it was clear that the time had come for the former prisoners to make their ways home. The Mortalon forces would soon learn what had happened and send soldiers toward the mines. But an alliance had been formed, an alliance among all the many peoples who had never united before. It looked like there would indeed be some change coming to Wyrd World.

And for the three humans and one dit-dit who belonged on a different world, it was time to leave as well.

CHAPTER ELEVEN

# MADE FOR A SEQUEL

We made our famous author sit down and think calmly and carefully about where he wanted to go.

"Think about your hotel room," Maggie said as we huddled on the dusty rock floor. "Think about the pictures on the walls, the bedspread, the little ice bucket."

"And," I added, "be sure you think about it as it was just before you left. Your bed was messed up, remember.

It was early evening, getting dark outside. Think about a story where we three have this great adventure but come back to your hotel room just moments after we leave. That way none of us will have to explain where we've been."

"Though later you'll probably want to buy yourself a new blue bathrobe," Maggie suggested.

"Okay," P.L. said. "I think I've got the hang of this now."

He turned to our Wyrd World friends, who were staring at us curiously. "Best of luck with your rebellion," he said, shaking hands (or what passed for hands) among them. "I'll try to keep in touch with lots of sequels."

"Is that some sort of wizardly magic?" Toraleen asked.

"I guess it is," the famous author laughed. "The magic of writing."

Maggie hugged Toraleen, and the two bubbled about how absolutely awesome the other was. I couldn't quite hug slimy Oooloop, but I gave him a solid pat. Then Roosh and Reesh engulfed us all in giggly wispy hugs until we finally pulled away, and Maggie stuck the staff into the circlet on P.L.'s head.

The transfer was as dizzying as always, but I was so

happy to end up in that hotel room I could have knelt and kissed the rug. P.L. sat with a grunt on his unmade bed. He took off the silver circlet and handed it to me. "Without a doubt, this has been the most . . . interesting author visit I have ever made."

"You don't want to come back and use the circlet again sometime?" Maggie asked.

"No, no, that's all right. It was fun, in a terrifying sort of way, but from now on, I think I'll live my adventures in my head and on the page." Then he laughed. "You know, authors sometimes wonder if we aren't a little crazy, thinking up all the weird stuff we put in books. It's comforting to know that we're not any crazier than the real universe is."

Looking at Maggie, I suddenly realized how totally filthy we were, to say nothing of the fact that we weren't wearing the same clothes we'd left for school in. Looking at me, she must have had the same thought.

"Hey, if famous authors can think up entire worlds, we can think up some explanation for looking like this," Maggie said.

"Or sneak in before Mom and Dad see us," I suggested. "But we'd better get going."

I turned to P. L. Cuthbertson and shook his hand. "I look forward to reading your next book, sir."

"And I look forward to writing it. You two really do have the stuff of heroes, you know."

As Maggie and I walked home, those words repeated in my head. I'd never thought I was the heroic type. And really, I'm not. But in books, the main character has got to do what the story calls for him to do. And as it turns out, books and life really aren't very different at all.

A Wyrd thought but a true one.

# ABOUT THE AUTHOR

Pamela F. Service has written more than thirty books in the science fiction, fantasy, and nonfiction genres. After working as a history museum curator for many years in Indiana, she became the director of a museum in Eureka, California, where she lives with her husband and cats. She is also active in community theater, politics, and beachcombing.

# ABOUT THE ILLUSTRATOR

Mike Gorman is a seasoned editorial illustrator whose work has been seen in the *New York Times*, the *New Yorker*, *Entertainment Weekly*, and other publications. He is also the illustrator of the Alien Agent series. He lives in Westbrook, Maine, with his wife, three children, a dog, a cat, two toads, and a gecko.

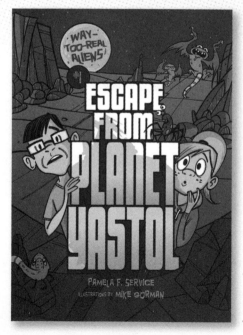

## JOSH IMAGINED THE PERFECT VACATION PLANET— BUT IT'S ABOUT TO BECOME WAY TOO REAL . . .

### #2 THE NOT-SO-PERFECT PLANET

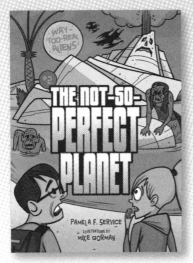

Josh Higgins has an alien gizmo that lets him think his way to other planets—and he does NOT want to use it. But Maggie won't stop bugging him, so he agrees to an off-world vacation. Josh dreams up a planet full of blue oceans and white beaches. But a parade of cranky creatures soon spoils Josh and Maggie's perfect getaway.

The planet's locals just can't get along, and Josh and Maggie find themselves caught up in the squabbling. Will the Earth kids discover a way to keep the peace? Or will Josh and Maggie become prisoners of the not-so-perfect planet?

## JOSH SAID HE'D NEVER VISIT ANOTHER ALIEN WORLD. THEN HIS FAVORITE WRITER CAME TO TOWN . . .

### #3 THE WIZARDS OF WYRD WORLD

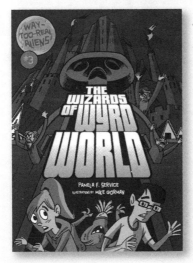

Josh and Maggie have vowed not to use their alien gizmo. But when the famous author P.L. Cuthbertson, Josh and Maggie prepare to visit the land of Cuthbertson's books: Wyrd World.

As soon as the crew arrives, some of Wyrd World's locals mistake P.L. for a wizard—and that's not a good thing. Josh and Maggie begin a rescue mission, sneaking through fortresses and dungeons. But to challenge the planet's evil rulers, they'll have to unite a group of rebels and outcasts who would just as soon fight each other. . . .

**#3**

**alien expedition**

PAMELA F. SERVICE

illustrated by mike gorman

Zack and Vraj have a mission in Mongolia: explore the area for traces of dinosaurs . . . the lost ancestors of an alien race?

**#4**

**alien encounter**

PAMELA F. SERVICE

illustrated by mike gorman

Zack's out to find a lost alien boy at the Roswell UFO festival. When Zack's dad goes missing too, can Zack save him without blowing his cover?

**#5**

**alien contact**

Zack has a new mission, and a new ally . . . who's maybe kind of cute. Can they stop evil aliens from sabotaging the Galactic Union?

**#6**

**alien envoy**

PAMELA F. SERVICE

illustrated by mike gorman

The Galactic Union is sending Zack on his first trip back to outer space. And the future of Earth is at stake.